T0193646

WEAKFLESH

YOLANDA KEY

authorHOUSE®

AuthorHouse™
1663 Liberty Drive
Bloomington, IN 47403
www.authorhouse.com
Phone: 1 (800) 839-8640

Published by AuthorHouse 09/24/2018

ISBN: 978-1-5462-5992-3 (sc)
ISBN: 978-1-5462-5991-6 (e)

Library of Congress Control Number: 2018910847

Print information available on the last page.

PREFACE

Have you ever wondered what it's like to be a foster child? I myself could not imagine the situation, but it is quite common. We will never know what it is like unless we live it ourselves. Foster homes are provided to offer a good life to children, and in certain cases, they do. In others, they do not. Trying to raise a family comes with its ups and downs. We want what is best for our children when we are focused on what is right, even though we sometimes do not know exactly what it is.

Take a home of six: a mother, a father, and four children. It's a family full of love and ambition and a strong background of always helping others to make things work but never once thinking that the society will take their whole world and crumble their close bond. The father was named Joseph, and the mother's name was Anita. They had loved each other since grade school and never thought of anyone else taking the other's place. Love is never blind when two people love each other; nothing and no one can take its place.

CHAPTER 1

Anita was a homemaker, while Joseph was the breadwinner. He was a hardworking man, and she was a hardworking woman. They would go days at a time without seeing each other but never thought about the absence of companionship.

One day, Joseph was on his way to work when he stopped at the local coffee shop to get a cup of coffee, like he always did to get his day started. A woman of such beauty and striking curves—with a gorgeous smile, long hair, and glistening skin, with this magnificent smell of perfume—walked in. Joseph really wasn't paying her any attention because all he could think about was his family and how he never got to spend time with them. There were so many other guys whistling and winking at this woman. One was brave enough to ask what her name was. She replied, "My name is Anita" with such a soft, elegant sound.

Now, that got Joseph's attention, because his wife's name was also Anita. This Anita did not act as if she was interested in all the other guys in the shop, but she did have some interest in Joseph—all because he did not raise a brow about her presence.

Anita walked up to Joseph and said, "Good morning, sir. How are you this lovely morning?"

Joseph replied, "Good morning" with a smile as he began to get his change from the cashier to leave the store.

Anita felt rejected and said, "I did not catch your name."

He replied, "Joseph," and went on about his day.

As Joseph walked out the door, he was a little puzzled because the woman had to have seen his wedding band and there were so many other guys trying to get her attention. Joseph just thought, *Oh well. It's none of my concern.*

Joseph got in his truck and drove to work.

That evening, as he was walking to his truck to go home, he saw a nice car with tinted windows riding slowly by his job. He had never seen this car around town. Since he was a local police officer, he paid close attention to the license plate. It was from Ohio. Before he could learn anything more about the car, it drove off.

Joseph was very eager to get home to spend time with his family, because it had been a long time since he had been able to do that. Joseph wanted to stop by the local market to get Anita some flowers to show how much he missed her and some chocolate candy for the children. So he stopped, and as he got out, he noticed the Ohio license plate in the parking lot. He said to himself, "I will finally see who this car belongs to."

Joseph walked into the market and everyone spoke to him, as they always did. He did not see any unfamiliar faces, so he went to the candy aisle to get the children candy and then to the floral department to get Anita her flowers. Joseph was hoping all the fresh tulips were not gone because those were Anita's favorite.

As he turned the corner, he smelled this soft perfume, and he knew he had smelled it before. There she was—the woman from the coffee shop—looking as ravishing as she had before. She had some yellow and white tulips in her hand, arranged so perfectly. She noticed Joseph and said, "So we meet again."

Joseph said, "Hello."

The woman said, "You're Joseph, right?"

Joseph said politely, "Yes, ma'am." He then said, "I'm not sure, but I think the guys said your name is Anita. That is also my wife's name."

Anita smiled and said, "Well, I see you have good taste."

"Thank you. My wife loves tulips, too."

Anita said, "Oh really?" She then held out the beautiful flower arrangement to hand to Joseph.

Joseph said, "I cannot take your flowers, although they are beautiful."

"I insist, since we share the same name and we like the same flowers. She deserves these."

Joseph saw that Anita was not taking no for an answer, so he took the arrangement, thanked the young lady, and went on his way.

Anita watched Joseph as he walked away. She looked at him with eyes of lust and fornication. She did not break her gaze until he was out of sight.

Joseph was finally on his way home to see his family. He was so excited, even though he was a little late. Joseph drove up in the driveway. He saw his wife's figure in the doorway and smiled as if it was their first meeting.

He got out, and his wife opened the door. His wife and children waited for him to come in with lots of hugs and kisses.

Suddenly, they heard a horn as a car drove by. Everyone turned around to see who it was, but the car was going so fast they missed it.

Joseph closed the door and enjoyed his family for the rest of the evening.

The morning came, and Joseph awakened with his beautiful wife lying in his arms. He said to God a prayer of thanks for his family. Joseph finally finished praying and lay there kissing his wife on her forehead. Then he heard a horn blow again—the same sound he'd heard last night when he was in the doorway. He thought, *Could it be? Nah, I don't think this lady is stalking me.*

His wife awoke with a smile and asked him, "What is wrong, honey? You have a puzzled look on your face."

He paused and said with a smile, "Oh nothing, baby. Good morning."

Throughout the whole day, Joseph was not as focused as he usually was, but he enjoyed his family for the rest of the weekend.

Finally he was back to his long hours at the police station, while his wife, Anita, was at home being the homemaker.

Life throws its twists sometimes when the devil has his opportunity to step in. Joseph had a long day at work. Exhausted, he went into the station to take a nap before he drove home. That's when it all started.

He clocked out and went to the rest area in the back of the station. He sat in the recliner, got comfortable in the chair, and leaned his head back. One of his coworkers came to the door. "Joseph, there is this young lady at the desk asking for you. And she is very upset."

Joseph asked, "Who is it?"

The coworker said, "I don't know, but she is hot. Man, I know you're not creeping on Anita!"

Joseph got up from his comfortable spot and went to see what she wanted. As he walked to the desk, he smelled that perfume again. He thought, *I know this is not this woman again. What could she possibly want?*

The woman said with great emphases "Joseph, thank God you are here. I need your help." Fear was in her eyes, and tears were rolling down her face.

Joseph said, "I am sorry. How may I help you?"

"Can we talk privately?"

Everyone was looking with suspension, wondering why she was asking for Joseph and who this peculiar woman was. He took the lady to one of the interviewing rooms. The woman walked in front of him, twisting her hips and smelling ravishing. Everyone was watching her as she walked away, even the females.

Joseph said, "What seems to be the problem?"

Anita came out with it. "It's my ex-husband. He won't leave me alone. I have moved away from him as well as taken restraining orders out on him, but he just won't stop."

Joseph said, "I see."

Anita looked at Joseph as if he wasn't concerned, as if he did not have a care in the world. She got up out of the chair and was more upset. Sniffling and crying, she stated, "All you men are the same. You don't care."

Joseph went to the door and apologized for his behavior. He told her he was very tired. He asked her, "Why did you ask for me? You know nothing about me."

"Well, from what I hear in town, you are a well-known officer, and you try to do what is right."

He said, "Why, thank you," but still was not persuaded, still wondering why she had come by his house blowing her horn.

Anita sat back down and began to talk some more about her problem. Joseph listened, and she began to feel better.

It was way past the time for Joseph to go home, so his wife Anita called and asked was he ok? Joseph replied, "Honey something came up, but I will be home shortly. I love you," and hung up. Anita stated she was sorry she had kept him so long and that he needed to get home to his loving family. She thanked Joseph for listening and said that she felt better already. Joseph said that the officers would keep a lookout for this guy and if she had any more trouble to give him a call. Joseph handed her his business card, with his cell phone number on it. He thought this might be a mistake, but he gave his card to everyone who needed help, so it should not be a problem. He escorted the lady out of the room and got his things to leave for the day. Joseph walked the lady to her car and said goodbye. She thanked him again, and they went their separate ways.

Joseph rode home with all types of thoughts running through his head. Why did this lady keep appearing in his life? He finally made it home and was glad to get there. His oldest son, Columbus, said, "Hi, Dad. How was your day? We missed you."

Joseph stated, "I'm sorry I'm late. How are you doing, son? How is school. You doing well in sports? Dating anyone?"

Columbus went on and on about his activities, and his dad listened carefully, saying he was sorry for not being there like he should have been.

They went in the house to see the rest of the family. His wife, Anita, seemed different tonight. She was not talking that much, but he couldn't put his finger on why.

The family sat down to the dinner table and said grace. They enjoyed their dinner. When the children finished, the two girls, Lisa and Alisha, twin sisters, cleared the table, while the two boys, Columbus and Craig, took out the trash. All the children knew something was not right. They were not used to their mom being this quiet. The children asked to be excused, kissed their parents goodnight, and went to bed.

Finally, Joseph and Anita were alone. The room was quiet and still. The only thing you could hear was the furnace from the basement. Anita had a disappointed look on her face. Joseph did not know what to say.

"What's wrong, honey?" he asked quietly.

Anita remained quiet for a minute. "How was your evening?" she finally asked.

Joseph looked deep into her eyes. Something was wrong. He had likely disappointed her by coming home so late without calling.

Anita said, "I'm just gonna go to bed." She kissed her husband on his cheek and turned away, but as she turned, she had a flashback from her past, from when she was younger. She screamed. In a panic, Joseph immediately went to her side, asking her what was wrong. The children came running out of their rooms.

Anita really did not know what to tell her family, but she knew she needed to lie down. Joseph took Anita by the hand and escorted her to their room. The children walked behind her to make sure she was all right. Anita convinced the children she was okay and they could go back to bed. Joseph kept close to Anita, not leaving her side. He closed their bedroom door and started apologizing for being so late.

Anita was very weak. She knew that something was not right. She told Joseph she didn't understand why he had been so late. She had never known him to do this. She was not stupid! Joseph assured Anita that it would never happen again. It was just something that came up at work, and he could not get out of it.

"Baby, I am sorry," he said. He would take off tomorrow to make sure she was okay. Anita told him that he didn't have to do that and that she would be okay. Joseph said he had to because he was tired anyway, and it would give them some alone time, since the children would be in school. Joseph lay in bed and held Anita the whole night, while Anita cried herself to sleep.

CHAPTER 2

The next morning, the smell of bacon, eggs, and biscuits was in the air. The children knocked on their mom's bedroom door and kissed her goodbye before they went off to school.

Anita was feeling much better, assured that everything was going to be okay. Joseph came into the room with a tray full of breakfast and some fresh tulips clipped onto the tray. Anita smiled when he entered the room. Joseph said grace, and they had breakfast in bed.

They were almost finished eating when Joseph's phone rang. It was a strange number. He did not want to answer, so he ignored the call and told Anita this was "her day."

Anita smiled, and they held hands. "Baby," she said, "I am not used to you being so distant from me. You know how it was when I was coming up."

Joseph placed two fingers across Anita's lips and told her in a calm voice, "Baby, shhhh. Be quiet. Let's not think of negative things." He removed the tray from the bed, closed their room door, turned the radio on to some Aaron Hall, and turned the lights down low while the fireplace knocked the crispness out of the room. He went to the bed and started massaging Anita's hands, then her arms and shoulders, nuzzling her neck slowly and gently. The track on the radio changed to one of their favorite songs. They both recognized it as they looked deep into each other's eyes. They began to kiss passionately, very slowly and gently, as if it were their first time. The energy coming from both of them was so strong, they both knew this was long overdue.

Anita caressed Joseph and whispered sweet nothings in his ear, telling him softly how good he was making her feel. Joseph was moaning with great pleasure. He was ready to enter Anita's hot climate. He took his time, teasing her lips, which were plump and ready to take his stiff rod. It was so hard you would think it was full of iron, like a locomotive running off the tracks. His rod was finally beginning to coast, and it was right at the entrance. Anita's lips, tired of getting teased, reached out and grabbed it. She took a deep breath, and Joseph clenched his butt cheeks to keep him from exploding. As he entered, it was a straight shot. Although the walls of Anita's cave were closing in, he was getting more and more excited. Anita began to roll her hips, as she had gotten used to Joseph's rod. Joseph began to stroke slow and easy, not too fast; he didn't want this experience to be breezy. Anita was trying to hold back. She didn't want Joseph to see her wild side, so she slowed down. Joseph began to go faster, and Anita couldn't take much more, so Joseph turned Anita around and began to start hitting her on her caboose. Anita began to throw it to Joseph like she had never done before. This experience was so good!

Joseph cried out, "Oh shit, baby, you never have done this before!"

Anita began to scream. She was getting wetter and wetter. The friction between them was getting unbearable, and they both climaxed as if it were their last.

Anita was smiling, and Joseph was too. They could not believe what they had been missing. They looked at each other and grinned and began to make love all over again. After a couple of times more, they were exhausted. They lay across the bed and held each other tight. Then they took a long nap before the children got home, knowing it would be a long time before they would be alone again.

CHAPTER 3

Columbus pulled up in the yard, excited to see his dad's car home. He ran into the house to give his dad a big hug. As he walked in the door, he could not hear a sound. He walked upstairs and knocked on his parents' door. No one answered, so he cracked it open and peeked inside. He saw his mom and dad fast asleep. He closed the door, trying not to make a sound. However, his dad was roused from his sleep.

"How was your day, son?"

Columbus replied, "Oh, Dad, I didn't mean to wake you."

"It's quite all right. I was about to get up anyway."

Anita woke up next. "Oh my, what time is it?"

Joseph said, "Hi, honey."

Columbus said, "Dad, you are not at work."

Anita was upset she did not have dinner on. "Don't worry about it, love," Joseph said.

Columbus jumped with excitement and thanked his father, and then they heard the sound of the other children's bus pulling up. Columbus ran downstairs to tell them the good news. Anita and Joseph looked at each other, and they both said at the same time, "I love you."

They got up to get ready for dinner before it got too late. The children were so happy. It had been a long time since the whole family had been out together. They all agreed to go to a restaurant of their father's choice, Dolce, one of the finest restaurants in the valley. This restaurant was very elegant, and the food was spectacular. The children always wanted to go there because they heard all of their classmates talking about it.

Finally, they were all dressed and ready to go to the restaurant. They all climbed into the family vehicle and were on their way.

They stopped at a number of stop signs on the way. At one of them, an unidentified car pulled up behind them. The music it played was so loud that it vibrated the windows in the family vehicle.

Joseph said, "What is their problem?" He sat there for a few moments, and the car behind him honked its horn. Joseph remained at the stop, until the car behind them swerved around, then pulled off really fast. Joseph said, "I am not going to allow no one to spoil the family evening." He did not call it in, even though he figured something strange was happening because the license plate was an Ohio tag.

They finally made it to the restaurant, and the parking lot was full. Anita said, "I hope we will be able to get a table."

Joseph said, "Honey, don't worry about that. I know the owner. He will make room for us. He owes me a favor."

They finally found a parking spot, and they all got out and entered the restaurant. As they reached the door, the owner was greeting people. Spotting Joseph and his family, he prompted the hostess to find them the best table they had. Anita was impressed. The children were too, and it was smiles all around. The hostess sat the family near a fireplace, close to a waterfall filled with blue crystals.

The children were in awe. Anita and Joseph were too; they had never seen an atmosphere so luxurious.

They sat at the table, and then the hostess took their drink order. Anita smiled at Joseph. "Thank you, honey."

"You're quite welcome."

The hostess arrived back with their drinks and informed them that their waitress would be with them shortly. The family all thanked the hostess and held hands to pray.

As Joseph began to say grace, he smelled that perfume again. He opened one of his eyes to see if it was who he thought. "Oh, it's, Joseph!" coming from the woman's voice. He immediately closed his eyes to finish praying.

When the family had finished their prayer, they all looked up. The boys all had awestruck looks on their faces as they saw their waitress.

Anita, Joseph thought.

She looked the family over and said, "Hi, Joseph," giving him a peculiar look.

Joseph's wife looked at the woman and politely said, "I am Anita, Joseph's wife."

"Oh, in that case, Anita," the waitress said, "I *know* who you are. Joseph, you have a lovely family. Thank you again for the other night."

The children and Anita looked at Joseph, their mouths hanging open. Anita the waitress asked the family to take their orders. Joseph did not know what to say. He asked Anita the waitress to give them a minute. Anita said, "Okay," and walked away.

Joseph said, "It's not what you guys think." He tried to downplay the awkward situation, but his family regarded him suspiciously. Anita the waitress was in her designated area, but she kept looking at Joseph.

Joseph's wife suddenly began praying, tears streaming from her eyes. She asked to be excused, and she went to the bathroom to get herself together. The daughters both went with her to make sure she was okay. Joseph did not know what to say or do. He was just speechless. He knew he had let his wife down again.

CHAPTER 4

Anita burst through the bathroom door and locked herself in one of the stalls, sobbing. Her daughters ran behind her, desperately trying to calm her down, letting her know everything was going to be okay. Anita was not hearing it. She began to have flashbacks about her past. It was an experience she did not want to relive—the pain, the agony, the turmoil of her childhood—it was unbearable for her to fathom again.

Alisha and Lisa did not know what to say or do; they pleaded with their mom. Anita just knew her past was coming back to haunt her. The things she had gone through in her past could have been prevented, if only her parents had fought for what they believed in.

Anita finally pulled herself together and stepped out of the stall.

Back at the table, Joseph and the boys were sitting very quietly with puzzled looks on their faces, not knowing what to say. Joseph finally broke the silence, using a strong, firm voice. "Now, boys, listen here …"

Neither Columbus nor Craig wanted to hear what their father had to say, thinking he had hurt their mother. Columbus just starred at his father, while Craig held his head down, looking so disappointed.

Anita and the girls came waltzing back to the table with smiles on their faces, as if nothing had happened. Anita looked at Joseph, and Joseph immediately asked for the manager to get another waitress for their table.

"What is wrong?" the manager asked.

Anita said emphatically, "The waitress is flirting with my husband."

The manager apologized and went over to Anita the waitress to inform her that she would not be serving their table anymore. Anita looked at the table and did not create a scene; she just complied with what her manager had told her. Then the manager assigned a waiter—a very handsome one, Anita noted—to the table. Anita did not look at him in a lusting way even once, having eyes only for Joseph.

The family ordered their food and continued the rest of their evening with lots of laughter and joy. The girls, Lisa and Alisha, could not eat all their food, so they asked for takeaway boxes. The waiter went to get them and left the check for them to pay. Joseph was stunned as he looked at the check. The manager had written a message: "This one is on me." This made Joseph quite happy, as it was quite an expensive bill. Not wanting the family to know, he placed his credit card in with the bill and left a fifty-dollar tip for the waiter, along with a note of thanks for rescuing them.

The family was ready to go, so they gathered their things and stepped outside. The girls were laughing and teasing each other about how full they were when they noticed some loud noise coming from outside, near the family car. It was the vehicle they had seen at the stop sign earlier. Joseph again noticed the Ohio license plate. The guy seemed drunk, and he was calling, "Anita!" at the top of his lungs. "Anita, baby, please. I am sorry," he kept yelling.

Joseph told the girls to get in the truck. He was going to call the office to report a disturbance.

Anita, Joseph's wife, said, "That has to be embarrassing."

Anita the waitress came storming out the door, screaming, "Please, leave me alone, Charles. It's over between us. Why won't you leave me alone?"

"That's what I had to help her with the other night," Joseph said.

Anita said politely, "We will talk about this later."

They made their way home to enjoy the rest of their evening. As he started driving, Joseph called in the disturbance. The children were knocked out before he topped the hill on their way home. He turned on some slow music, and he and Anita listened in peaceful silence all the way home.

When they arrived home, the children were still sound asleep. They woke them up so they could go in for the night. Lisa and Alisha kissed their parents and thanked them for a wonderful evening. Craig and Columbus hugged them as well and went into the house. As Joseph and Anita got dressed for bed, Joseph felt that he needed to apologize again. Anita stepped close to him, put two fingers on his lips, and said, "Let's just remember this evening like it is."

They climbed into bed and held each other until the break of dawn.

CHAPTER 5

The morning came, and the two awoke just as they had gone to sleep—holding each other. Anita said excitedly, "Good morning, dear!"

"Good morning."

All of a sudden, Anita began to feel tightness her chest. She had not felt this before, so it scared her. She did not want to startle her husband, so she didn't say anything to him about it. She went downstairs to make sure the children had gotten off to school all right, and sure enough, they were already gone. She began to make Joseph his morning coffee and toast and she went to grab the newspaper. Anta laid everything out on the table for Joseph so when he came downstairs it would be waiting on him.

Joseph finally made it downstairs with a puzzling thought in his head from last night hoping, praying that his wife had forgotten about everything and they could go back to their perfect little life. Joseph sat at the table pretending to read his newspaper with all types of thoughts in his head, sitting across from his beautiful wife of twenty years.

Anita sat there looking as if she had seen a ghost, trying to hold back the pain, but all the thoughts of her past were coming back to haunt her. Anita did not know what to say or do, but she did know she needed to get to the bottom of this. I guess that's what you call a woman's intuition—doubts that arise when some things have changed.

Joseph finished his breakfast, kissed his wife goodbye, and made his way to work. Anita watched Joseph as he was pulling out as if she were never going to see him again.

Soon she began to feel a little better, but she remained bothered by the unwelcomed questions. She began to pray, as hard as she could. She prayed for answers, because she knew something was not right. She asked God for a sign, a sign to allow her to see what was really going on.

She decided she would get dressed for the day and have a picnic with her husband in the park. Anita pulled out her red dress, the one that clung so nicely to her caramel body. She put on her favorite perfume from Victoria's Secret and some three-inch stilettos, then headed to the

market to fill the basket for the surprise picnic she would prepare for Joseph.

When Anita got to the market, she was the center of attention. No one recognized her, which wasn't surprising, as she hadn't dressed that way in a long time. As she waltzed in, she left a tantalizing scent behind her. The ladies eyed her with jealousy, and the men lusted after her. After gathering all her market items, she went to the odds-and-ends store to pick up some extra supplies for the picnic. Then she went to the station, not really knowing what she expected to see. Anita sat in her Mercedes and waited almost until noon. There was no activity.

Inside the station, Anita the waitress was trying to get another restraining order against her ex-husband. She went to the desk and asked for Joseph.

When Joseph heard about it, he put his head in his hands, exasperated. He did not want to get in the middle of anything else with this woman. It was putting him in a bind and making his wife feel a

certain way that was making things very uncomfortable. However, the waitress insisted that she talk to Joseph, and she wasn't taking no for an answer. Joseph finally came out of his office to see what the ruckus was about. Anita saw Joseph and said emphatically, "Finally, you are here. Thank God."

Joseph said formally and politely, "Ma'am, how may I help you?"

"It's my husband—well, ex-husband, that is. He won't … ah … leave me alone. I have done everything." She began to cry.

Joseph wasn't buying the act one bit. All he could think of was how she had left him in a bind with his family at the dinner table. She began to get louder, and the other guys in the station started feeling sorry for her, not knowing she was putting on an act to get her way. Anita was really laying it on thick, so Joseph decided to take her to his office to try to calm her down. The waitress followed behind him. Joseph asked her to have a seat.

"Now, tell me, what is really going on here? What's the real reason you want out of this man's life?"

The waitress kept going on and on about how he was so mean to her and how he kept accusing her of sleeping around and she was tired of it. Then she started talking about her sex life with her ex-husband. They would play this seductive role-playing game that involved tying her up, but sometimes he would be too aggressive. Anita stated she had been happy at one point in their marriage, but had become too overbearing and controlling, and she could not take it anymore. Then she moved closer to Joseph and began telling him what type of man she was attracted to.

Joseph loosened his tie, and he started sweating bullets down his forehead. He had never had a woman this close to him besides his wife. The other officers were peeking through the glass, acting like children, as if they'd never seen this type of behavior from a woman before. Anita

began to bite her lips. She smelled sweet, like fresh fruit ripe from the vine. Joseph was trying hard not to give in to this loose woman. After all, he was happily married.

As Joseph continued asking questions, he began to stutter. Anita was so close to him now, right up against his neck, smelling him.

"I usually don't flirt with men," she said, "but when I want something, nothing can stop me from getting it."

There was a knock at the door, and someone poked his head in telling Joseph he had a visitor.

Distracted, Joseph said, "Who is it?"

"Um," the officer replied, "*Mrs.* Anita."

Joseph cleared his throat. "Is something wrong? Keep her busy for a minute, please." Now Joseph didn't know what to do. He told the waitress, "Please do not ask for me anymore. One of the other officers will have to help you."

He stepped out of his office and looked around the corner. He could not believe his eyes. It was his wife, looking ravishing. As he approached her, she smelled fresh and floral like a bed of roses. Her three-inch heels made her legs look like a million bucks.

"Anita?" he said with a questioning look on his face.

"Joseph," she said, breaking into that sunshine smile of hers. She had a picnic basket on her arm. "I've come to take you for lunch." Joseph was very surprised. Anita had never done this before. She turned to walk out the double doors, and Joseph followed.

Anita the waitress was behind them, but his wife never once turned around to see her there. With a smirk on her face, she whispered, "I'll be back."

CHAPTER 6

Anita and Joseph stepped into the Mercedes and left for the vineyard and their picnic. Joseph did not know what to say or do; all he could think about was the rush he felt getting caught with that succulent woman up against his neck, smelling the way she smelled. The adrenaline rush reminded him of the way he used to feel back in the day.

"What is wrong, honey? You are in a daze," Anita asked.

Joseph played it off by saying, "I can't believe you are here. You look amazing."

Anita looked in the rearview mirror and saw the waitress walking toward her car. She said to herself, *Hmm, so that's the problem, huh? I'm going to fix this once and for all.*

She smiled at Joseph, and they headed to the vineyard. When they arrived, Joseph got out and opened Anita's door. She got out and began strutting along the trail to the picnic area. Oh, my God. There were so many people looking at Anita, whispering how beautiful she looked. Joseph was sort of jealous, but he wouldn't show it, because he knew she was going home with him. They arrived at the picnic area, and Joseph laid out the blanket and helped his wife with everything.

Anita began to forget about the offense she had taken earlier. She was at peace being with her man. Joseph was happy as well. He was surprised, but he made sure he gave his wife his undivided attention. Other couples were there as well, some serenading each other and some massaging each other. It was just a happy and pleasant day. Anita looked into Joseph's eyes and began singing their favorite song: "Let's Get It Together," by 702.

Joseph couldn't say anything. Everyone stopped what they were doing and began to listen to Anita sing. Joseph grabbed Anita by the hand. A tear streamed down his face, and he started singing to her, "Maybe I Deserve," by Tank. At the end of the song, Anita and Joseph got a standing ovation from the onlookers. They were so into each other that they barely noticed the audience they had won over by the sounds they were giving to each other. They just looked into each other's eyes and began to lust, thinking about making love. Their minds were so full of passion, something they had not felt in a long time.

Joseph saw a woman peeping at them from behind one of the vines. He believed it was Anita the waitress, but he could not make her out because of the scarf she was wearing around her head.

Anita and Joseph enjoyed their lunch, but soon it was well past the time for Joseph to go back to work. He did not want to end this great moment with his wife, so he called into the station to inform the guys he was taking the rest of the evening off. His partner informed him that a Miss Anita Eubanks had left fifteen messages for him to call her.

"Man, I'm not trying to get in your business, but this woman is going to ruin your marriage," his partner helpfully informed him.

Joseph paused to gather his thoughts. "Thanks, man. I'll make a note of that," he said, taking care to throw his wife off the scent of their topic.

Anita sensed he did not want her to know what they were talking about, so she just smiled and acted as if nothing bothered her.

Joseph got off the phone with his partner, and the couple went on with their day, getting through the rest of it without anything messing up their evening.

Early the next day, Joseph's cell phone rang. It had to be important, coming this early in the morning. As Joseph picked up the phone, it stopped ringing, then it rang again, this time only once. Joseph checked the caller ID—"Private." Who would be calling this early, and from a private number? He surely didn't know.

The ringing phone woke up his wife. Anita asked, "Hun, what's wrong?"

"Nothing, love. Go back to sleep."

Joseph turned off the ringer and waited for another call, but this time he went into the bathroom so he wouldn't wake Anita. Little did

he know that Anita was not asleep; she just lay there to see what he was doing. The phone rang, and Joseph answered, "Who is this?"

He heard some heavy breathing and a soft-spoken voice say, "It's me, baby."

Joseph recognized the voice. He didn't say anything at first, because he didn't know what to say. Finally, he asked, "What do you want from me?"

The voice responded passionately, "I want you, Big Daddy!"

Joseph was surprised—and quite flattered. His wife had never talked to him like that.

Anita rolled over in the bed and said, "Honey, are you coming back to bed?"

"In a minute … I have a stomach ache," Joseph lied. He thought, *What am I doing? Why am I lying to my wife?*

Anita was not buying the lie by a long shot. She got up and went into the bathroom, where Joseph was. As she peeped around the corner, she saw that Joseph was not even on the toilet. He was sitting in the lounge chair, on the phone, whispering, as if he was telling some a great secret. Anita burst into the bathroom, hollering, "I can't believe you! After all I've done for you, and you cheat on me?"

Anita was frantic and furious. She smacked the cell phone out of Joseph's hand. When it landed, she picked it up and turned on the speaker.

The voice on the other end said, "I better let you go. It seems like you are really going to get it." The voice continued, "You best to get a grip on your husband before I take him." The voice laughed, and the call disconnected. Anita began thinking about her past again. *It's over and can't no one stop it,* she thought hysterically. She began hyperventilating, breathing harder and harder, tears running down her face. Joseph didn't know what to do. He kept calling her name, but she wasn't listening.

Anita's head began to spin. With little oxygen getting to her brain, she fell to the floor, hitting her head against the toilet. Joseph ran to her rescue. He shook her, but she wasn't waking up. He called 911.

"It's my wife," he said. "She's fainted. You need to send someone right away." He began to administer CPR, but Anita wasn't responding. She was turning blue!

Finally the ambulance got there and began their procedure. Slowly, Anita regained consciousness, but she was very tired. "Anita," Joseph said, "baby, are you okay?" The paramedic asked him to step back until they were finished.

Just then, Joseph heard the bus pull up.

Oh my God, it's the children.

CHAPTER 7

The girls ran into the house to see what was the matter. Alisha was the first to speak. "It's something Dad has done."

"Don't say that," Lisa said. "Dad would never do anything to hurt Mom."

Columbus and Craig had not made it home from practice yet, but the girls knew they would be worried, so Alisha took it on herself to call Columbus's girlfriend to arrange for them to come to the hospital when they got out. The ambulance took Anita to Vineyard Memorial for further observation to make sure Anita was all right. The hospital was full, as usual.

Joseph pulled into the ER area and rushed in to be with his wife. Anita was in a room in the waiting area. The doctor had just arrived and examined her. His observation showed that she was very stressed and needed some rest. She also showed that she was anemic. Joseph began to feel down and out. Columbus and Craig arrived, looking less than happy, asking what was wrong with their mom. Joseph could not say anything; he was so lost for words.

The nurse came out and told the family they could see her now. The children all went in, and the doctor remained outside and told Joseph that perhaps she needed some psychiatric help from a counselor because she seemed really stressed.

Joseph did not want to go in the room. He did not want to face his children because he did not want to see the disappointment on their faces. Meanwhile, in the room, Anita began talking to the children, albeit weakly. The nurse suggested that Anita to take it easy. She had suffered a serious fainting spell, and perhaps a concussion, and they did not want her to go through that again.

Joseph finally worked up the nerve to go in the room with the rest of the family. He walked in with his head held down. "Hi, everyone," he said quietly.

Craig stated in a strong, disrespecting voice, Dad, how could you allow this to happen?

"Yeah, Dad," Columbus added, "what is really going on?"

The girls stood by their mother's bedside to comfort her, making sure she didn't get upset again. The boys and Joseph begin to argue, not thinking clearly about the situation.

Anita bolted upright in bed. "Stop it, stop it, stop it, I say! We are a family, and we are going to work through this with God's help!"

The boys and their dad began to calm down. Anita began sharing her feelings: "I never thought this would happen to me. I have been happily married for twenty years. I don't expect everything to be peaches and cream all the time. We all have to go through things for us to learn. My mom died from stress, and I promised myself I was not going to let anything or anyone take over my life, unless that was death itself."

Tears started streaming down her face. "I miss my momma and all because Satan and a loose woman took away my family. That is all I have to say!" Anita then asked the family to hold one another's hands

and begin to pray. "Heavenly Father, I know you are a forgiving God and you will not put more on us than we can bear, but I ask you to come by my house, move throughout my family, and have mercy on us, because without your protection and your strength, the devil will defeat us. We ask this not because we are worthy but because we need you and we can't fight this battle by ourselves. In Jesus's name, we pray. Amen."

There was a knock at the door. It was the doctor, coming in again to check on Anita and to let them know that she could go home tomorrow, but she needed plenty of rest. Anita was getting tired, so the children kissed her goodnight and went outside the room to give their dad some time with her.

Joseph grabbed the Anita by the hand, and he began praying silently to himself. When he finished, he looked at Anita and said, "Baby, I'm going to fix this. I am so sorry." He kissed Anita on the forehead and exited the room.

When Joseph and the children arrived home, they couldn't even talk to each other. Alisha stated, "It is not the same without Mom around."

Joseph didn't say anything. He still did not know what to say. He hadn't done anything with that woman, but he couldn't deny that lust had been in his heart. If he had been firm with her from the beginning, none of this would have happened. He got up out of his lounge chair, kissed the children goodnight, and went to bed.

The children stayed up, talking about how their grandmother had died. Alisha and Lisa had not known the truth, thinking their grandmother had died from old age. Columbus and Craig said that they hadn't known either. They all agreed that they needed to help lighten their mom's load around the house and they would show her how much she meant to them all. They all hugged and went to bed.

The next morning, Joseph was up before the kids. The aroma coming from the kitchen made it smell like a Saturday morning when his wife was home. The kids all ran into the kitchen, yelling, "Mom is home," but when they got there, it was their dad that had the kitchen smelling so good. The children said and asked when they were going to pick up their mom.

Joseph said, "As soon as you all sit down and enjoy your breakfast. Then you'll get dressed, and we are all going to the hospital—together, as a family."

Columbus saw a sparkle in his dad's eyes, so he did not make a fuss.

"Dad, I'm going to get your morning paper," he said.

"Dad, we are going to set the table," Lisa said, speaking for both girls.

Craig said, "I'll help with whatever else you need me to do, Dad."

Columbus went to the door. Outside, by the mailbox, there was a stuffed bear and a balloon bearing the message, "Get well soon." Columbus said, "It must be from the neighbors." He did not open the card; he just grabbed the newspaper, the bear, and the balloon, and took them all into the house. Columbus said, "Dad, look what the neighbors left for Mom." They all agreed that this was very nice.

They sat at the table, said grace, and had a lovely breakfast. The children were so anxious about seeing their mother that they all chipped in and cleaned the kitchen together. When they had all finished, they went upstairs to get dressed for the day.

Joseph was curious about who had left the bear and balloon, so he picked up the card. "A New Friend" was written on the envelope. Joseph stood in the kitchen, looking puzzled. He opened the card. On the inside, it said, "Thanks again, my chocolate teddy."

Joseph was enraged. He knew it was from that psychotic waitress. He turned on the gas stove and burned the card, leaving the bear and the balloon.

The children were all dressed and ready to go. Lisa said, "Dad, you're not ready."

He said, "I am, baby girl. Let me change my shirt."

The whole family got in the truck and headed to the hospital. When they arrived, Mom was waiting to see them. She was sitting on the bed as they all walked in. The children ran in to give their mom a hug. Anita was excited to see the whole family because it had been quite some time since she had been away from them all. Joseph finally walked in after meeting with the nurse about his wife's care at home before she was discharged. He walked to his wife's bedside, and tears rolled down his face as he looked deep into his wife's eyes.

"Honey, I love you."

Anita stood up and gave Joseph the biggest kiss and hug in front of the children, not caring if the children would tease them. She wanted him to know that she understood him and loved him as well.

Finally they gathered Anita's belongings and left the hospital. The girls were talking their mom's head off, and the boys were doing the same thing to their dad. It seemed just like old times for them all. Joseph and Anita did not have a problem with all the aggravation because they knew their children were happy.

Anita said loudly, getting everyone's attention, "I'm sorry I have been such a burden to everyone, but I am scared, and I don't know what to do." She began to cry, and Joseph pulled over to the side of the road and got out. The children didn't know what he was doing. Neither did Anita. He walked to Anita's door, opened it, and started praying, holding Anita's hand tightly, ensuring her that everything was going to be okay. When Joseph stopped praying, Anita stopped crying, feeling better now.

CHAPTER 8

When they arrived home, an investigator was standing in the yard.

"Joseph, who is that?" Anita asked. Joseph stated that it was one of the investigators from his job. "That's strange. He could have called you on your cell."

The children all helped gather their mom's things while Joseph helped her into the house.

Alisha said, "Mom, you rest tonight. We will cook dinner." Craig and Columbus set the dinner table and took out the trash, and Joseph went back outside to talk to the investigator. The investigator's name was Sammy. Joseph and Sammy had worked on only one case together, and you couldn't exactly call them friends—far from it.

Very formally, Sammy began, "So, Joseph where were you last night about seven o'clock?"

Joseph hesitated a moment before responding suspiciously, "Umm, why do you ask?"

Sammy said, "Well, since you asked, some allegations have been brought against you that I do not think you will like."

"I was at the hospital with my sick wife, Anita—"

"Anita, hmmm ..." Sammy said

"And my children also. My wife fainted yesterday and had to be taken to the hospital by ambulance."

Sammy said, "Well, since you have an alibi, there is no use taking you downtown for questioning."

"What the hell does that mean?"

"Well, a woman by the name of Anita Eubanks claims you tried to rape her."

"What? What do you mean I tried to rape her? When?"

"Supposedly last night, around seven."

"My God, man, I know we haven't seen eye to eye in the past, but you have to believe I would never do anything like this to anyone."

"No, we don't 'see eye to eye,' but I have to do my job."

Joseph said, Man, keep your voice down. My sick wife will hear you.

"Well, Joseph, it is best not to keep secrets from your wife. Tends to cause more problems in the long run."

Joseph looked at Sammy with an evil eye. "Sure," he said derisively. "Is there anything else?"

"I will be getting back to you real soon." Sammy hopped in his vehicle and left.

Joseph walked back in the house to his family. Joseph and his family had a quiet evening together, and they all climbed into the king-size bed and watched Lifetime movies until everyone fell asleep.

In the middle of the night, Anita jumped and began to scream as if someone were chasing her. She woke everyone in the room, scaring the fire out of the girls as well as the boys.

"What is wrong, honey?" Joseph said.

Anita's eyes were frantic. "I don't know. I had a dream that the house was on fire."

They all looked around at each other and began sniffing the air. There was no mistaking it. They smelled smoke. They all jumped up to see where it was coming from. Joseph was also frightened, not knowing what to do. They looked all over the house and noticed that the fire had gone out in the fireplace—that's with the smell was coming from. They all begin to laugh, realized they had gotten worked up over nothing.

Thanks to the excitement, they all got an early start to their day.

CHAPTER 9

Anita began to feel better. The family went about their routine without a worry in the world. Life seemed to have adjusted back to normal. Anita was going to counseling and was having a breakthrough daily. She was not as stressed, and she did not feel as if she would lose her family again.

That is, until one day, when Anita was leaving her counseling session and needed to stop at the market for some milk. She got out at the local market and went inside. She went down the dairy aisle and got the milk, but the jug she picked up was leaking. The stock guy in the store area came out to help Anita clean up the milk that had spilled on floor.

The guy said, "Sorry, some of the milk jugs get damaged when we restock the shelves."

"Oh no, it's my fault," Anita said. "I should have paid attention when I picked up the jug. If you will give me a mop, I will clean it up."

The clerk laughed. "Oh no, it's my job to keep it clean and stocked back here."

Anita looked the guy in his eyes and noticed his name tag: "Charles." Anita said, "I have a cousin named Charles, from the States."

Charles said, "From the States? I am from the US. I came here to get my wife. Her name is Anita."

Anita said, "My name is Anita too—what a small world!" They both laughed. Anita told Charles it was nice to meet him, he said the same, and she walked away.

All types of thoughts went through Anita's head. She could not help but wonder, was this the drunk guy at the restaurant, Dolce, that night of the family dinner? It couldn't be, she thought. This man seemed too professional to do something like that. Anita checked out and went home to cook dinner. She listened to her self-help CD all the way home.

CHAPTER 10

At the station, Joseph was having a hard time because of the false accusations brought against him. Thank goodness he had an alibi. He had been at the hospital at the time of the event. Besides, no one in town really knew this woman, so no one could figure out where this had come from.

Charging through the station doors, the waitress Anita burst in all loud and out of order. "Where is the justice in this town? If I were in the US, this man would not be working for local citizens!"

An officer in the station asked Anita to keep her voice down, saying he would help her as much as he could. Joseph heard her from his office, so he came out to see if he could reason with this strange woman. He felt safe now that there were witnesses around. Joseph asked, "Anita, why are you doing this? You know I did not try to rape you."

She said, "You did. You tried to rape me *in your mind*."

Everyone looked stunned.

What! said the chief, having heard her statement. Oh, my God. I cannot believe you just said

He dropped the investigation against Joseph immediately.

Joseph received a phone call from Sammy. "Joseph," Sammy said, "I hear you have a stalker on your hands".

Joseph smirked. "Well, Sammy, at least we have all that behind us. Now you can get off my back."

Sammy said, "I apologize, man. I was just doing my job. Have a good day," and he hung up.

Joseph walked out of his office, his head held up high. He grabbed his jacket and headed for home. He sat in his truck with a smile on his face and, finally, with relief in his heart. Finally he had put all this behind him.

Joseph's phone rang. It was his wife.

Anita said, "Honey, could you bring some dinner rolls? I forgot them when I was at the market today."

Joseph replied, "Why, sure I can. Is there anything else you need?"

"I think that will be all—besides waiting on your handsome face to walk through the door."

Joseph smiled and said, "I will see you when I get home."

A few minutes later, Joseph's phone rang again. This time it was Anita the waitress.

"Wait, please don't hang up!" she said,

"Listen, Anita, I'm tired of you trying to ruin my marriage—as well as me. Goodbye."

"Wait, I'm sorry. It's just … I want you … and I need you, and it is hard for me to accept the fact that you are married."

Joseph said, "Well, I am, and I am happily married. I don't need you messing up things for us. Besides, I don't even know you."

"Well, it's done then," Anita said, "but one more thing. I just want to know, do you find me attractive?"

I am not going to answer that.

"For real, I just need to know, because I am so lost as to why you won't give me a chance—besides the fact that you are married."

"I am married, and I do not need your lies destroying my marriage. Good day, ma'am," he said, and he hung up.

Anita was pissed, but she did not call back. She wanted Joseph to think it was over and that she was going to leave him alone.

CHAPTER 11

Joseph arrived at the market to get the rolls. As he walked in, he bumped into Charles. Charles seemed to be in a hurry, so he said, "Excuse me," and walked out the door.

Joseph said to himself, *That man looks familiar.* He walked in to get the rolls and checked out at the register. Usually, Joseph would take the long way home, but this time he took a shortcut to get home faster. Joseph was going about 55 mph, listening to some Bob Marley, when he came up to a car beside the road with emergency lights on. It had a flat tire. Joseph didn't see anyone in or near the car, so he kept going. As he topped the hill, there was a woman walking. She was wearing a hood, to keep from being cold, he assumed. She was carrying some hills in her hand, and she was trying to walk as fast as she could.

Joseph knew his wife and children was waiting on him, but he was a police officer and was supposed to help civilians. Joseph slowed down and asked the lady where was she headed and if he could give her a lift. The woman stopped and said, "Why, sure."

Joseph said, "Hop in. I will give you a ride to where you are going."

The lady opened the door and got in the truck. She then closed the door, and Joseph turned the radio down some more. "Is that your car with the flat?" he asked.

The lady said with her head still covered with the hood of her jacket, "Yes, it is."

"My name is Joseph. I am a police officer from the vineyard."

The woman said, "Okay."

"I did not get your name."

"The woman took off her hood and said, I am so glad you stopped, Joseph. I was afraid if you knew who I was, you were not going to stop."

"Well, isn't this 'bout a bitch," Joseph said. "Anita, I can't believe I cannot get rid of you for nothing!"

Anita said, "I am not as bad a person as I may seem. We just got off on the wrong foot. If you just give me a chance to get to know me, we could be great friends."

Joseph came back with such anger in his voice, "I do not want to be friends with you. I just want to be rid of you once and for all." Anita held her head down and did not talk anymore. Joseph said, "Where do you live?"

Anita said, with her head still hung low, "Rosetta."

"Rosetta? That is too far."

Anita said, "You offered me a ride! Just put me out right here. I will get home the best way I know how!"

Joseph realized that Anita was getting mad, so he told her just to calm down. "I will take you home."

Joseph began to speed, as he was already late for dinner. Anita just sat on the passenger side of the vehicle, not making any movement. She began to sniffle, disappointed in the way Joseph was acting. Joseph turned the stereo up to keep from hearing Anita's sighs. As they got closer to the town of Rosetta, the streetlights became scarce because they were so far in the country. The paved road was ending, and as soon as they got onto the dirt road, it started to rain. The road was already muddy, and there was a trail from other cars that had entered the road. Anita hollered to inform Joseph he was driving recklessly. Joseph turned the music down and said, "What is your problem, ma'am? I'm taking you home. What more do you want?"

Anita replied, "I just want to get home alive, that's all."

Joseph saw he was scaring Anita, so he slowed down. The rain began to come down harder, and it was nearly pitch dark now. There was a small light coming up nearly at the end of the road. Joseph asked Anita how far they would have to go.

Anita replied, "Not much farther."

The tires on Joseph's truck began to slide, and Joseph tried to slow down, but he didn't do it fast enough. The truck began to hydroplane. As Joseph fought against it, Anita was hollering. She slid closer to Joseph out of fear.

The truck crashed into a tree. There was a lot of heavy breathing from fear, and Anita and Joseph both asked each other at the same time, "Are you all right?"

Anita replied first, "I'm okay. I'm just a little shook up."

Joseph stated, "I'm fine also," but with a smirk.

Anita was puzzled. What's your problem?

Joseph stated, "Oh, nothing. It's just that we are both grown adults and we should not allow things in our life to make us act out of character."

Anita was surprised Joseph said that, so she didn't reply. She just smiled. They both got out of the truck and looked to see what the damage was. The tire was flat, and the fender was busted. There was no fixing this right way. Joseph went in his pocket to see if he had cell phone service yet. As he tried to make a call, the phone died, so he asked Anita to check her phone. She said, "My phone died back when he found her side the road. We can just walk to my home from here."

It began to rain again. They were both getting wet, so they jogged the rest of the way. They finally arrived at Anita's front porch. Anita noticed the light on the porch was off. "There must have been a power surge," Anita said. Anita opened the door and tried to turn on the light switch. It did not turn on. Joseph began to wonder what his wife must be thinking right now. He knew she would worry, so he asked the waitress how long the power was usually out. She replied, "About a couple of hours." Joseph sighed.

"Oh shit, my wife is going to be pissed."

Anita said, "I am sorry."

Joseph said, "I bet you are. I can't believe you tricked me again."

"Tricked you again? What do you mean? Do you think this was intentional?" Anita began to show a side of her that she never had before. "Excuse me, Mr. Joseph, you are not all that. I'm so sick of you scolding me and blaming things on me. You did not have to stop and give me a ride. You did not have to take the time out and listen to me. Part of you was curious as to what I was about. I made some part of you feel a little younger. You liked the attention, didn't you?" Anita began to get closer to Joseph, with her seductive eyes and plump lips. She was very flirtatious as she talked to Joseph, and some part of Joseph was weak. He did not want to do anything with this woman, but he was weak in her presence. He was getting excited listening to the things Anita was saying. She came closer and closer, their lips almost touching. Joseph pushed away immediately. All he could think of was his family, which he loved so much.

"Stop! I am a married man. I love my wife and my family, and you are not worth losing them."

Anita looks at Joseph with fiery rage. She glanced at a lamp on her table, then ran over to it, pulled it out of the wall, and threw it at

Joseph. Joseph ducked just as it sailed over his head, smashing against the wall behind him.

"Woman, are you crazy? What are you trying to do, kill me?"

Anita, still filled with rage, started crying and screaming. She was distracted by some lights streaming through the window. Before she could grab anything else to throw at him, Joseph ran up behind her to hold her down.

They both heard footsteps on the porch. Anita cried out, "Help, he's trying to rape me." The door busted open. It was Anita's husband, Charles. Anita screamed, "Charles, I'm so glad to see you! This man is trying to rape me."

Charles said, "Really, Anita, you expect me to believe that? I am so sick of you doing this to people. You picked this man of all men, a devoted husband and father."

Joseph was surprised that this man was saying this to his wife.

Anita said, "Leave me alone. You know nothing about me and my new love."

Joseph spoke up. "Your new love? How you could say that. I promise you, I have nothing going on with this woman, sir. I was just trying to give her a lift because she was broken down up the road. It really is sad that you can't help people."

Anita started screaming in outrage, "All you men are the same. You all stick together. I'm so sick of you all. All I tried to do is go on with my life, without all the pain, to forget about all the unwanted feelings I had with you, Charles." Anita began pacing around, getting herself more and more upset.

CHAPTER 12

Back at home, Anita was beginning to get anxious. What was really going on with Joseph, and why he had not arrived yet? She told the children to go ahead and set the table and maybe their dad would be home momentarily. The fireplace was still burning in the den, and she could hear the rain coming down pretty strong. The children began to talk amongst themselves, hoping and praying that their dad was going to be okay in this stormy weather. It was getting late, and the food was getting cold, so Anita instructed the children to go ahead and eat their dinner. Their father must have gotten stuck in that bad weather, she said.

Although Anita said this to the children, in the back of her mind, she was not so sure. The children said their grace and thanked one another for dinner. Anita did not have much to say at the dinner table, so she asked the children if she could be excused. She needed to lie down. The children knew their mom was worried about their dad, so they did not pick a fuss with their mom's wishes. Anita left the dinner table slowly and walked upstairs to her room. The children cleared the table and begin talking amongst themselves.

Craig and Columbus were sort of quiet. They did not want their mom to hear their opinion about their dad. Alisha and Lisa begin rambling, upset. They could not understand why their dad was treating their mom this away. They both knew something was not right, and they said they were going to get to the bottom of it. Craig and Columbus both agreed that they needed to leave that to the grown-ups and it had nothing to do with them. Columbus said, "We just need to pray about it and God will work it out."

Unbeknownst to the children, their mom was listening to everything they were saying she began to pray, "Heavenly Father, I do not know what is going on with my husband and why I am going through this, but Father, you know what is best, and I will leave it all in your hands. In Jesus's name, I pray. Amen!"

Anita waited until the children were in bed, sound asleep. Then she got dressed to go look for her husband. *Some women may think it's not worth it, but if you know that God has given you the right mate, you will go to great lengths to keep him, overlooking pride and putting those feelings aside so you can be real and have a happy life.*

Anita eased out of the house slowly, being as quiet as she could. She got in her car and stared searching for her husband. All types of unwanted feelings and thoughts went through Anita's mind as she rode the highways, searching for her husband, but nothing could overpower the thought of her loving him, despite his flaws.

Anita searched all the roads she knew her husband might be on. She searched them high and low but could not find any sign of her husband's truck. Finally, she came to an abandoned car with its lights flashing very low, as if the battery was about to go dead. She did not see anyone in the car, and it was no car she was familiar with, so she passed by it slowly. Anita was curiously, thinking who this car might belong to. There was no sign of anyone close by it. She made a U-turn in the middle of the road to go check it out. She came close to the car again, and she noticed it had an Ohio license plate on it.

"Hmm, that is strange," Anita said. "I don't recall anyone having those plates in town. Maybe it's someone new to the area."

Anita pulled up behind the car and scoped out the scene before she got out, to make sure it was safe. As she got out, she smelled one of her favorite perfumes, so she knew it was a woman that had been stranded. Anita walked closer to the car and looked all around it. She wanted to open the door, but she knew that would be trespassing. She looked around to see if anyone was looking, and she pulled on the door handle to see if it was unlocked. The door opened slowly, and she looked around to see if there was anyone looking. She was tense and kind of scared. She sat down slowly in the seat of the car, smelling a strong Victoria's Secret fragrance that she herself loved: Dream Angels. She then knew it was a female's car.

Anita was paranoid that someone would catch her. She looked around in the car to see if she saw anything familiar. She pulled the visor down, and a sheet of paper fell in her lap, as well as some pictures—pictures of her home her children and pictures of her and her husband together when they were in the vineyard on their lunch date. Anita's face was scratched out, and there were hearts all around Joseph's face.

Anita became anxious and started breathing heavily. She felt an anxiety attack coming on, but she wanted to get down to the bottom of this, so she did not allow it to control her. She opened the glove compartment so she could see who this vehicle belong to. She looked and looked, but she could not find the insurance and registration. She kept on digging, but still nothing—until she thought of the console in the middle of the car, which she was leaning over. Anita eased back in the driver side seat and slowly opened the middle console. She fumbled through the console and found the insurance card and registration. It had two names on it. The names were Charles and Anita Edwards.

Anita, she said to herself.

She thought back to the restaurant. The waitress that was flirting with Joseph was named Anita! She became furious and started breathing heavily. She thought to herself, *I'm going to kill them. I cannot believe he would do such a thing to me.*

Anita slammed the console down and grabbed the insurance card, which had the address. She stormed out of the car with such frustration and anger. She slammed the door, breathing heavily, and began to become overly anxious. Anita sat down in her own car and began to pray, "Heavenly Father, I need you right now. I need you to help me sort this out, because I refuse to allow this situation to beat me as it did my parents. In Jesus's name, amen!"

She took a few deep breaths to get her anxiety under control. Then she counted backward while exhaling slow breaths to get her oxygen back on the right level. She waited, then opened her eyes and starting thinking this situation through. She thought to herself, *Now that I have control of my thoughts, the next thing to do is get some answers.*

Anita put the address in her GPS to find out where this woman lived. She was familiar with the roads, because it was near the venue where she had picnicked with Joseph. She followed the directions, and soon the streetlights ended—she assumed from the storm earlier in the evening. Anita followed the directions slowly, until she came up to her husband's truck. The truck was wrecked into a tree.

Anita began to panic, thinking there was something wrong with Joseph. She stopped her car to check if he was in the truck, and as she approached, she smelled the strong scent of perfume. She immediately assumed that Joseph was having an affair. There was no sign of Joseph or anything, only some boot tracks in the mud and a smaller high-heeled shoe.

Anita ran back to her car and continued to follow the GPS directions. Finally, about four hundred feet from her destination, she saw there was this small log cabin back up in the trees. It looked like a nice, cozy home. Anita crept up in the driveway and saw another truck there. She got out of her car quietly to keep anyone from hearing her. She softly stepped up on the porch, and she heard some people talking. She did not recognize the voices, but they sounded very angry. Anita kept listening, until she heard Joseph her husband say, "I need to get home to my family."

"Honey, I am here!" she cried out frantically.

Joseph replied, "Anita, come in please."

Anita tried to enter, but the door was locked.

Joseph started begging with the couple, "Please, let my wife in."

The waitress replied, "No, she will never, ever have you. She finally needs to know the reason why her life has changed."

Charles interrupted, "Anita, you need to leave these innocent people alone."

The waitress became more frustrated. It seemed everyone was against her now, and she did not know what to do. Anita walked over to the door to unlock it, but she had a look on her face that puzzled Joseph, as if he was not sure he wanted her to open the door.

Anita, Joseph's wife, had her cell phone in her pocket, and she pressed record. Charles told his wife as she walked over to the door, "Honey, I love you, and I all I want is what's best for you and me." Anita hesitated a moment, not saying a word.

Joseph tried to reason with the waitress by saying, "When someone loves you and they have done all they can and have not given you a legitimate reason why they do not, you should believe them."

The waitress began to feel something strange in her chest. She did not know what she really wanted. She just knew that something was not right. She grabbed her chest and began to take deep breaths. She felt as if she was having a heart attack.

Joseph's wife turned the knob, trying to get in. She screamed, "If you don't open this door, I am going to bust it down."

The waitress said, "Hold on, I am going to open the door!"

Slowly, she opened it.

Joseph was so happy to see his wife, but his joy was short-lived, as the waitress reached into her pocket and pulled out a small gun. Charles screamed, "No!"

"If I can't be happy, no one will be happy!"

Joseph's wife began crying, and she said a silent prayer: *Father, God, please help us out of this situation, for you know what is best.*

The moment Anita finished her prayer, a beam of sunlight shone through the shades of the window. Tears begin falling from the waitress's face. It was as if she had a deep thought in her head that she did not want to keep doing this but her actions proved different. The waitress began to tremble with the gun in her hand, with a look of regret on her face. She started to scream and cry at the same time.

"Why am I doing this? It doesn't make any sense. Why am I crying? Joseph is my man, and we will be together, no matter what any of you say." She looked at Joseph with lust in her eyes, turned to his wife, and pointed the gun at her.

Joseph yelled, "No, please, please, Anita, listen to me! I know you are confused right now, and you don't know what you want to do, but just think about the consequences of your actions and listen to your inner thoughts. I love my wife and my family, and I will do anything to protect them. If it is me that you want, let them go and we can be together."

Joseph's wife fell right into character. "Yes, you can have him. Just don't kill me. I have my children to think about."

Anita slowly dropped the gun to her side. Then she turned it on her husband, Charles. She spoke slowly. "You did this to me. You are the reason for all of this. If had never cheated on me, I would not be reacting this way!"

Joseph said to Anita the waitress, "Never allow someone else to be your downfall. He is not worth it. Besides, you said you wanted us to be together, and now it is time."

Anita threw the gun on the floor. It went off. The bullet flew past everyone. Anita the waitress ducked for cover, but the bullet ricocheted off the steel fireplace and hit her square in the forehead. She instantly fell to the floor. Everyone was as quiet as they could be. Joseph's wife Anita began to check herself to make sure she had not been hit. Then she jumped up to check on Joseph. Joseph must have hit his head on something, because blood was trickling down the side of his face.

Anita Joseph's wife cried, "Wake up!"

Joseph was out of it. His head had taken a hard bump on the end of the coffee table.

Anita the waitress lay there moaning faintly. She had no one to check on her. She was dying slowly as the blood began to flow from her body. Her head leaned to the side, her eyes wide open. She said, very faintly, "I am finally free," and she died.

Charles just sat in the corner and cried out, "Someone, please, help me." He was losing his mind. He never once went to his wife's side.

Anita and Charles got up off the floor and began to walk away. As they approached the front door, Anita looked back at Charles and said, "We have to be careful of our actions in life. We never know what effects they have on the next person."

Joseph was very weak. Anita put him in the car to take him to hospital. As she closed the door, she heard another gunshot. Anita cried out, "Lord, have mercy," got in her car, and drove her husband to the hospital.

As Anita approached the emergency room door, the attendant ran to assist her. The attendant said, "Officer Joseph, oh my God!"

They put him in a wheelchair and begin to examine him. Anita called the police and told them they needed to send a coroner to the address and that she and her husband were at the hospital getting checked out. She had recorded the entire situation.

Later that night, Joseph was checked out, and so was his wife, but only after it was discovered that Anita was pregnant. Joseph was happy, and so was Anita. They went home to tell the children the good news.

When they got home, the children ran outside to greet their parents to find out where they had been. They had never both stayed away from home like that and not called or anything. The children saw their dad's bandage wrapped around his head. "Dad, what's wrong?" Columbus asked.

Joseph said, "It's a long story." He didn't want to talk about it now, but he did want to let them know they would have another brother or sister coming soon. "When your mom was having those fainting spells, turns out she was pregnant."

They helped their dad into bed, and the whole family slept in the same room that night. The next morning, the children prepared breakfast in bed for their parents. They brought them the newspaper, and on the front page was the story. The town recognized Anita as a hero for protecting her husband. Anita looked at Joseph, and he looked back at her, and they said to each other, "I love you."

The children said, "We love you all too."

They all hugged each other, and they lived happily ever after.

ABOUT THE AUTHOR

Yolanda was born in Colquitt, Georgia. She is the eldest of four siblings. Yolanda grew up in a town close to Colquitt called Donalsonville, where she graduated high school in 1996. She pursued a career as a nurse assistant, which allowed her to provide for her two sons for many years. Yolanda was married but always felt as if she were single due to the horrible life she had with her children's father. So she moved to Dothan, Alabama, to get away from the abuse and neglect she encountered with her husband.

She continued to work as a nursing assistant at Wiregrass Hospice for five years, until she found the desire to become a professional truck driver in 2006. Yolanda also attended Troy University, where she aspired to become a community counselor. Yolanda volunteered and helped individuals in her community. She also started a community group called The Community Inspirations in 2011, where she recognized the first African American commissioner in the Wiregrass.

Yolanda always loved to write short stories and poems throughout her life. So she decided one day she wanted to write a book and have it published. Yolanda wanted her first book to be inspirational but also to be about something that many people struggle with today—the desires of the flesh. Yolanda is very conservative, so she didn't know how to get her book published until one day she had an epiphany and stepped out on faith to start the process of getting her book published in 2017.

Printed in the United States
By Bookmasters